This book belongs to

_____

_____

_____

To Michael and my wee lassies – R.C.

For Derek and Oscar – K.M.

Picture Kelpies is an imprint of Floris Books. First published in 2014 by Floris Books. Ninth printing 2017. Text © 2014 Rebecca Colby
Illustrations © 2014 Kate McLelland. Rebecca Colby and Kate McLelland assert their right under the Copyright, Designs and Patents Act 1988 to be recognised
as the Author and Illustrator of this Work. All rights reserved. No part of this book may be reproduced without prior permission of Floris Books, Edinburgh
www.florisbooks.co.uk. The publisher acknowledges subsidy from Creative Scotland towards the publication of this volume. British Library CIP Data available
ISBN 978-178250-048-3 Printed in Malaysia

Rebecca Colby & Kate McLelland

There was a Wee Lassie who swallowed a Midgie

Picture
Kelpies

There was a wee lassie who swallowed a midgie.
I don't know why she swallowed the midgie,
so teeny and squidgy!

There was a wee lassie who swallowed a trout;
it flip-flopped and swim-swam and bubbled about.

She swallowed the trout
to catch the midgie;

I don't know why she
swallowed the midgie,
so teeny and squidgy!

There was a wee lassie who swallowed a puffin.
As if it were nothing, she swallowed a puffin!

She swallowed the puffin
to catch the trout,

that flip-flopped
and swim-swam
and bubbled about.

She swallowed the trout
to catch the midgie;

I don't know why she
swallowed the midgie,
so teeny and squidgy!

There was a wee lassie who swallowed a Scottie.
Completely dotty, she swallowed a Scottie!

She swallowed the Scottie
         to catch the puffin,

she swallowed the puffin
   to catch the trout,

that flip-flopped
   and swim-swam
      and bubbled about.

She swallowed the trout
   to catch the midgie;

I don't know why she
      swallowed the midgie,
so teeny and squidgy!

There was a wee lassie who swallowed an eagle.
It's really not legal to swallow an eagle!

She swallowed the eagle to catch the Scottie,

she swallowed the Scottie
to catch the puffin,

she swallowed the puffin
to catch the trout,

that flip-flopped
and swim-swam
and bubbled about.

She swallowed the trout
to catch the midgie;

I don't know why she
swallowed the midgie,
so teeny and squidgy!

There was a wee lassie who swallowed a seal.
Like no big deal, she swallowed a seal!

She swallowed the seal to catch the eagle,

she swallowed the eagle to catch the Scottie,

she swallowed the Scottie
              to catch the puffin,

she swallowed the puffin
           to catch the trout,
that flip-flopped
       and swim-swam
            and bubbled about.

She swallowed the trout
      to catch the midgie;

I don't know why she
        swallowed the midgie,
so teeny and squidgy!

There was a wee lassie who swallowed a cow.
I mean – wow! – she swallowed a cow!

She swallowed the cow to catch the seal,

she swallowed the seal to catch the eagle,

she swallowed the eagle to catch the Scottie,

she swallowed the Scottie
        to catch the puffin,

she swallowed the puffin
        to catch the trout,
that flip-flopped
        and swim-swam
            and bubbled about.

She swallowed the trout
        to catch the midgie;

I don't know why she
        swallowed the midgie,
so teeny and squidgy!

There was a wee lassie who swallowed a Nessie.
It's especially messy to swallow a Nessie!

She swallowed the Nessie to catch the cow,

she swallowed the cow to catch the seal,

she swallowed the seal to catch the eagle,

she swallowed the eagle to catch the Scottie,

she swallowed the Scottie
              to catch the puffin,

she swallowed the puffin
          to catch the trout,
that flip-flopped
        and swim-swam
            and bubbled about.

She swallowed the trout
    to catch the midgie;

I don't know why she
    swallowed the midgie,
so teeny and squidgy!

There was a wee lassie who swallowed a loch.
It was massive but, och, she swallowed a loch!

She swallowed the loch to wash down the Nessie,
she swallowed the Nessie to catch the cow,
she swallowed the cow to catch the seal,
she swallowed the seal to catch the eagle,
she swallowed the eagle to catch the Scottie,
she swallowed the Scottie
        to catch the puffin,
she swallowed the puffin
        to catch the trout,
that flip-flopped
        and swim-swam
        and bubbled about.
She swallowed the trout
        to catch the midgie;

I don't know why she
        swallowed the midgie,
so teeny and squidgy!

There was a wee lassie who swallowed a midgie,
but why a midgie, so teeny and squidgy?

And could she have swallowed yet more? – no doubt!
But the loch that sloshed through her washed everything…

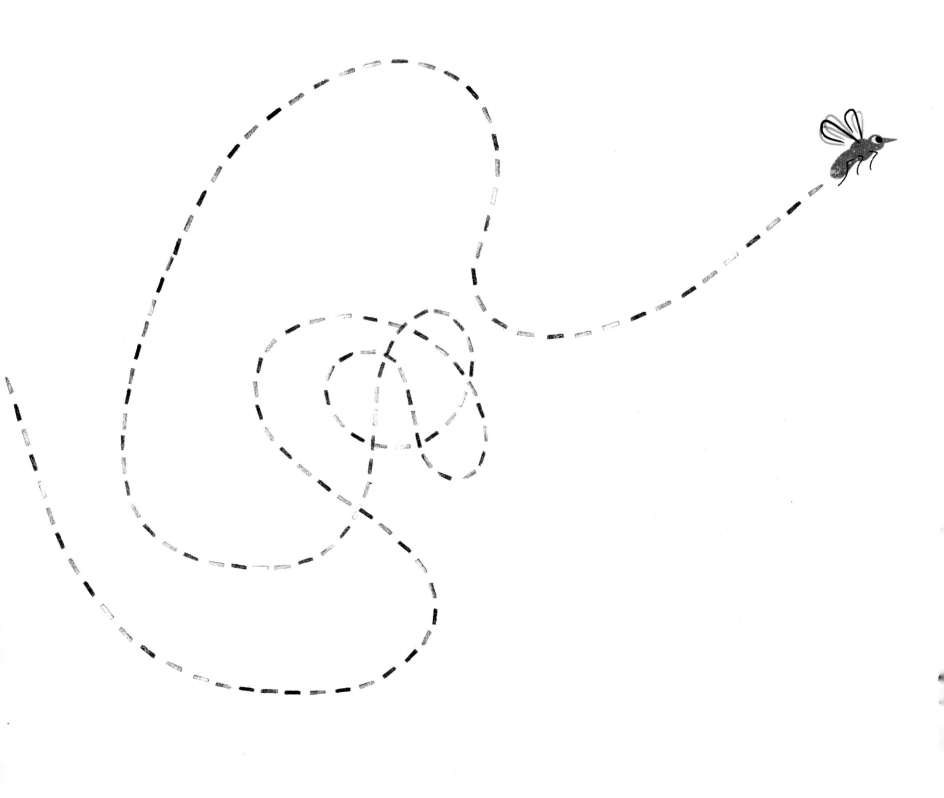